TO LOVE A LITTLE MORE

A COLLECTION OF SHORT STORIES

PRIYANGA M SRINIVASAN

ISBN 979-888591907-4

Contents

Acknowledgements

Many thanks to the higher power who made the book possible.

To my brother Thilipan, who encouraged me to take this adventure.

To my friends Mani, Manju and Annnu who provided me with constructive feedback. You guys are my support system and I love each one of you.

To my high school English teacher, Mrs. Grace Sheela, my inspiration behind my writing. You introduced me to literature and I've been in love ever since.

To all my friends, who believed in me and motivated me throughout my life.

Last but not the least, to all my readers, thank you. I hope you enjoy the book.

From the Author

During my school days I spent as much time as I could in the library. When many of my classmates were interested in screening the pages of popular magazines, I would grab a story book, be seated comfortably on the chair, right next to the garden and be lost in its pages.

Books introduced me to the outside world. I fell in love with landscapes, characters, plots and would imagine myself travelling with them in their journey.

Every book I read wasn't just a book, but a trip taken with the characters. This book was inspired by many such journeys in the past.

I hope readers find themselves in one such journey through this book. I would love to hear your feedback.

Regards,

Priyanga M. Srinivasan

mspriyanga@gmail.com

CHAPTER ONE

Under the Lamp Post

The light fell on the stone bench, placed right below it, and I decided to rest on it for a while. I was not ready to interact with the world tonight. The world had forgotten about me two years back when my wife died in an accident. I'm Patrick, an artist, a painter to be specific. After cutting my ties with friends and family, I stayed home all day. Now that my inspiration had passed away, I had nothing left to sketch. The company that hired me had lost its hope, it threw me out. It happened twenty-four hours before, I've been sleeping all day, but then I decided to take a walk.

With no destination in my mind, I walked where my feet roamed into the night. As I sat on the stone bench, life revisited me, every moment of laughter I spent with my love, my family, and all the sweet memories came back to me. I shed tears of loneliness, felt scared about the future. I was sure no one at this moment cared if I did not return home tonight. I was ready to take the leap into the dark side, my mind was racing, and I looked up at the sky with hope of finding a guiding star. Even the stars abandoned me, it was cloudy by now and started drizzling. People ran for shelter, but I had no will or any reason to stay dry when everything about me was bathed in pain.

I welcomed the rain, as it drenched me. I was sitting alone there, letting the rain to wash out my tears. I heard a whimper, I looked around. I spotted a tail right under the bench. A puppy was trying to find warmth beneath it. As I lifted him, he became comfortable in my arms. We stayed there until the rain stopped.

I ended up adopting him. He was the spark I was hoping to see thorough the cloudy sky. I wasn't sure if I found him or he found me that day, but he gave a reason to live on, to walk though many roads once again, to smile, and look forward another day.

CHAPTER TWO

CHOOSING MYSELF

"Two roads diverged in a yellow wood,
And sorry I could not travel both."

A poem by Robert Frost, it had always been stuck in my mind. I have wondered how people would react when given a similar situation. What kind of stories do they have? What decisions are they struggling to make? Do they seek help from friends or make those tough decisions all by themselves? The only tough decision I have had to make so far was what to eat for breakfast, my favourite Pongal and sambar made by my mom or chapati and chenna made by my pinni.

Hi, I'm Stella, an introvert, working at a publishing company. A girl who had her future planned out, she knew what her life would be like five years from now, the very HR question everyone isn't sure what to say. At that time my life was revolving around Steve, my love of eight years. I was going to marry him when I turned twenty-five, have four kids, and that was all I dreamt off. Until the day he decided to walk away.

It wasn't a slow, losing interest, walking away kind of relationship. I've known him almost all my life and we've been in fight many a time but have never thought of breaking up, not even once. So, when he walked away, it was a sudden blow to me. I was all alone and did not know how to deal with it. When I was trying to accept the fact that he had walked out on me, he came back, wanting to marry me. My mind went, "Wait, what?" He asked me to marry him, saying that it's just a misunderstanding and I was excited like a fool, once again.

Sometimes things don't work out the way we want. I was left to make a decision whether to choose him or go on with my life. To choose him meant getting married and having kids and then the same cycle of getting hurt now and then. But I knew what I was getting into. On the other hand, on the unknown road I did not have anything in sight, it was blurry, and I had no idea what it held.

Yet, I chose the latter. I was not ready to find the new me. I cried in bed all night, but the next day, I was up and running. I found little steps to tread on, I started writing again, and I did everything I wanted to try. I got back into reading habit. I was trying to talk with more people. I was forcing myself out there to hold it all together and every night when I came to bed the silence was deafening. I could hear myself screaming to be pulled apart, limb by limb, every vein to be plucked out of its place, bleeding, burning, just to get rid of this pain pulsing through my body. Yet every morning, I seemed to wake up empty, but still I was walking and talking. I did my best to put on a smile to the outside world. As days passed, I was smiling more, I did not have to pretend anymore. I was becoming happy and learning what I am capable of and I was pushing myself to my limits.

After two years of separation, I wasn't thinking of him. He rarely seemed to cross my mind and I was living my life. Soon with the help of my friends, I was able to publish my work.

A small leap that gave me confidence. I was a writer, I did not need to be defined by another person, I knew now that I could make it. I was finding myself one day at a time and the answer to the question, where do you see yourself in five years? I would proudly reply, "I'll be a bestselling author."

8

CHAPTER THREE

TURN OF EVENTS

It was nine in the evening. I knocked on the door again. I've been knocking on the door for the past five minutes and she hasn't opened it yet. It's been pouring outside and I was fully drenched, shivering, calling out her name. The wind wasn't helping either. I was cold. I knocked a bit harder and this time I heard the footsteps running towards the door. I walked straight to the washroom, still scolding Hela. After a quick bath and dressing up, I was hungry. The last meal I ate was around twelve in the noon. As I walked out of the room, I froze.

Hela stood in front of me, in a black linen dress. She was beautiful. I couldn't take my eyes off her. And for the first time, since I walked into the room, I noticed the dim lights, the mild music and candles on the dinner table. She held out a glass of champagne, as I took it from her hand, she grabbed me, pulling me close, she kissed me. I can smell her perfume, a mild lavender, her favourite. I noticed now, she's in high heels, the one I got her last week. She guided me to the table and we sat down.

Hela made her special recipe, meat ravioli. I devoured heartily. We chatted while enjoying our dinner.

She stood up, cleared our plates, and went away to bring desserts. My mood changed significantly since the evening and I felt stupid to have yelled at her while walking in. I stood up, wanting to help her bring the dessert, and as I turned around I couldn't hold my tears.

In front of me, kneeling to the ground, Hela was holding out a beautiful ring, the one that had been passed on to her from her grandma. She looked at me with a big smile and I couldn't move. I was over the moon. "Yes!, Yes! Yes!" I screamed loudly.

Fast-forward three months! At the altar along with friends and family, she was looking gorgeous in her white wedding gown. I, who'd never believed in fairy tales and happily-ever after stories, stood there spellbound. I realised she was my happy place. Our fairy tale had just begun.

Zooming out, the sign on the entrance, read, Emma ♥Hela.

CHAPTER FOUR

PICK-A-SHOE

"A good shoe will take you to good places". I read this quote when I was a little child. I've always had love for shoes. As I grew old, the number of shoes I had also increased. My name is Jordan. I have a whole closet filled with boots and sports shoes and a few worn-out pairs that I had no heart to give up, they just sat there as if they've gone into retirement after years of walking around.

After recently moving into a small neighbourhood, this was the first time I walked out to visit the nearby market. The market had everything from cookies to meat, laptops, and clothing stores. I was admiring a scarf displayed on a window and my eyes caught the shoe store next door.

"Pick-a-shoe", the name of the store made me a bit curious and I walked in, to have a peek. I realised all the shoes were refurbished, yet looked as good as new. I happened to watch a teenager at the counter trading her old shoes for the ones she picked out. And she did not pay a penny. I was baffled, as I walked up to the counter, I saw an old man seated at a table repairing the old shoes that a customer had left behind. I watched him as he took off the heel, peeled out the inner soles, started washing them and fixing and making repairs.

I asked him why he'd been doing all this hard work, when he could just sell the good shoes for a profit. The old man smiled at me. He moved away from the table, I realised he was seated on a wheelchair. He came near me and with a sparkle in his eyes pointed me towards the little girl hopping around in her newly picked shoes. "That smile right there is why I do it," he said.

As we began talking, I learned that his name was John, an army veteran who lost his legs in a car crash, three years ago. He went on to explain how a few weeks after the incident he started experiencing phantom pains and couldn't sleep at night. One day when he was strolling through the neighbourhood, he came across a homeless man, walking with just a pair of socks covering his feet. He felt pity and offered him his old shoes. The homeless man was so grateful that he started crying. He then told him how he was praying for a pair of shoes to show up to an interview the next morning, this moved John so much that he wanted to start a shoe shop for anyone in the need.

I was now looking at him with admiration. John looked me in the eyes and said, "The happy faces of people when they pick out their shoes, makes me forget all about my pain and cheers me up, and that's the reason why I started this shop and will have its doors open always."

I spent the next thirty minutes talking with him, getting to know more about the town and his life and the wars he had been to. Slowly I fell in love with the shoemaker and the little town. I walked home with a big smile on my face and a heart leaping in joy, to bring back an old pair of shoes, to trade the very next day.

CHAPTER FIVE

UNEXPECTED FRIENDS

Lucas and I have been friends for eleven years. Every time we are together, people think we're a couple. We have spent most of our college holidays together. Though we're from different colleges, Lucas was the one to pick up and drop me at my college before going off to his.

Eventually people started talking and teasing us, but we were least bothered.

Lucas was my best friend. He would give me advice and find solutions to my problems. He would take care when I was sick. Living in a different state from home, this was very much appreciated by me and my parents, who grew to like him.

I'm Jacey and the day I met Lucas was an unexpected one. It was the day of inter college competition and the guitarist in our band was nowhere to be found. We were panicking. At the last-minute a guy from the nearby band, Keet agreed to play for us. After the program had ended, we paid him and parted. As we were walking towards the canteen for lunch, we found Keet with his gang seated there.

A senior from their college walked to us and began ragging us, we tried to ignore him and have our meal, but he was insulting us and even dared to lay hands on my friend. At this point, we were getting ready to walk away when Lucas stepped in all of a sudden and helped my friend. He was muscular and taller than the senior, who chickened off, after receiving a few punches.

Lucas was Keet's friend. He was one of the cultural organiser. We later got to know that he was the one who requested Keet to help us after realising we had no guitarist during the program.

When the senior walked out, Keet's gang joined us for lunch and we chatted away like old friends.

Lucas was seated right next to me, and when we introduced ourselves, we realised our hometown was the same. Our accent revealed our identity and just like meeting an old friend, we were chatting for hours.

An unexpected meeting changed our lives forever. Ever since then, Lucas has been a part of my life and family. Eleven years later, we still meet often, and talk over the phone every day. Some people come into our lives just to show us how beautiful it can be. They make us believe best friends are like siblings born in different wombs.

CHAPTER SIX

LOST AND FOUND

Vivian wakes up every day and jogs for forty-five minutes. She takes the usual route that passes through a bakery. She does not eat cakes, but loves the smell of fresh bread. After getting a cup of coffee she walks back home. This has been her routine for the past few years, having taken up a 9-5 job at a company, it pays the bills and kept her going.

Something had changed that day, there were fewer people at the desks, the break room that was always filled with co-workers gossiping was empty. As she walked into her work space and logged in, she finds a mail from the HR requesting Vivian's presence at her office, and two minutes into their conversation, she said, "Vivian, I'm sorry we have to let you go." She was handed a pink slip. Many lost their jobs that day. It all happened so fast, having no time to react.

On the way back to her desk, she saw many cardboard boxes out, people were collecting their belongings, with sadness written all over their faces. She was at the verge of tears. She started collecting all her stuff before walking out.

Seated at the bakery, Vivian ordered herself a cake and milkshake. She looked at her account balance, which was only sufficient for the next few months. She had to take care of food, rent and other expenses which meant she needed to find herself a job soon.

There wasn't enough time to sit around and be sad. With that in mind, she got up and went home.

Vivian spent the next two weeks applying for jobs. But got no positive reply. She now realised they were cutting off employees in most of the firms and she had to start searching elsewhere.

Worried and distorted, Vivian decided to take a walk in the park. With no thoughts in mind, she walked for twenty minutes until she was tired and had to take rest. She found an empty bench and sat down, a family was enjoying their picnic not far away from her, they had a little kid who was running around and playing. After a while the kid saw a balloon stuck on the tree and wanted it, it was too high for the father's reach. When the father tried to explain, the little one broke out in tears. The nearby shop was outside the park, which roughly took thirty minutes of walk. The mom hugged the little kid and gave her some treats to stop her tears and it worked like magic. The next minute she was dancing around, licking her lollipop.

Vivian had a thought, she knew what she had to do, but she was reluctant not knowing if it would work. Too many questions ringing in her mind on the way back home. She assured herself that she can make it work, "I'm good at what I do! My heart was convincing my brain. But what if it doesn't work? Said the brain, why not? The heart responded. She knew she had nothing to lose, and decided that she would give it a try for a week and decided to take it from there.

On her way back home, she stopped by the store to pick up a few commodities for the job the next day. Early that morning Vivian woke up and started preparing for the day. Around ten A. M. she moved towards the park, found a nice place to put up a stall and started selling balloons. She sold ten balloons in the whole day. Vivian took a deep breathe. She knew she could do better. The next day, she went to the park in the evening, figured that's when most of the families come out with the kids. That day Vivian sold twenty-five balloons.

Next day, she took a spot deep into the park. A nice place where most of the families sat down for picnic, on that day, she sold more than fifty balloons in just two hours. She was becoming aware of the spots, the timing, and how the crowd would vary according to the days. Vivian started shifting places throughout the day. In the morning, she would camp outside the park, where parents were on the way to day care. In the afternoon she would take a small walk around the park selling balloons, and in the evening, she would settle on the usual spot, where the families enjoy picnic.

A month into the job Vivian had made a profit of two hundred dollars. She wanted to improve, so she went and bought herself a cart. She attached a pump along with the balloons. She also started selling hotdogs. This was working well for her now. With a few trials and errors, she made enough money to help pay her bills. Possibly, no one could throw her out this time.

Vivian was now looking forward to each day. She made quite a few new friends in the park and the little kids started calling her the balloon lady. Now and then, when she finds someone really sad, Vivian would offer them a hotdog and a balloon along with a smile. She would comfort them, ask them not to lose hope and hold on for a little longer. Vivian was feeling cheerful. She thought to herself, "Maybe, some endings are just the beginning for a new chapter in life."

DEAR BREEZE

Dear Breeze,

You've brazed through many a writer's table, crossed through their fingertips, learned their dark secrets but never leaked any of it. You've been the first breath of an infant, the last breath of the deceased. You've travelled with people on their best days and worst nights, lifted up spirits of a lonely soul. Guided weary travellers through haunted forests. You come to me every season, bringing with you the essence of life. In summer , you pass by with heart-filled smiles, bringing melodies from the bird singing in the wild. In winter too, you come through, chill as the lonely nights. On rainy days, you bring me, the smell of fresh earth, you remind me the simple moments that bring joy on this earth. On autumn days, as I take a walk, you've made me a carpet to trod on, you blow those leaves on my lap, show me it's okay to fall, as long as you move on. Falling too seems so pretty with you by the side.

Every time you visit my windowsill, you make the wind chimes go crazy, until I peek my head through the curtains and you tell me stories of where you've been. You've travelled through all lands, the mountains, and the valleys, the darkest forests and the abandoned trails. Every time you visit, you change my mood in an instant, echoing sweet melodies as you hop through my fence, you bring me stories from a far-away friend, tears of words untold, laughter of the wavering soul.

Dear wind, I wish you'd take me along on your adventurous journeys. Let me go wild in your embrace, let me echo sweet melodies for people in distress, let me steal away their sadness. Let me spread the kindness you have bestowed upon me, the sense of freedom that only you bring to me.

Your dear friend,
Scooby
(The dog who lives in the blue house)

CHAPTER EIGHT

THE BURROW

Under the grounds of Mrs. Wilsdone's farm lived a rabbit family. Papa rabbit, Mama rabbit, three elder rabbits and two younger ones. The papa rabbit and mama rabbit were busy in the day time, running above the ground to bring food for the family, while the elder rabbits taught the younger ones and watched the burrow.

Mrs. Wilsdone's farm had cabbage patches, carrots, chilli, bell peppers, and few more vegetables. Since the food was abundant, the family of rabbits decided to settle right underneath the garden.

The three elder rabbits were called Blue, Pink, and Grey. They helped with their parents to get food and were also being trained to find their own burrows someday. The elder rabbits always made sure to follow every rule of papa rabbit and would be in bed by six p. m. They never went out whenever they were warned by their parents. The little kids, Shade and Shadow, however, were mischievous and never obeyed their parents. They knew where to find food; hence, did not worry about the rules and thought their parents were being unreasonable.

They would not listen when Blue taught about safety precautions, and to mark their way back or when Grey pointed out how to escape from predators. Pink would always be on their back scolding the little ones when they forgot to close the burrow entrance. Shade and Shadow grew to hate thier parents and siblings. They wanted to run away and find their own burrow and live freely without having to attend classes and getting scolded by Pink.

They planned to run away before autumn that year and find a place in the nearby farm. One day when the papa rabbit and mama rabbit had gone out, the three elder rabbits were being busy and did not notice Shade and Shadow as they snuck out through the side burrow. Shade was in such a hurry to escape that they forgot to close the side entrance when they left.

Shade and Shadow ran into the farm and ate all the cabbage, taking a bite from every plant that was sown and when they were tired, they hopped in through the fence into the neighbouring farm, to find a place for the night. They did not know that the farm had a guard dog Susie. They had never met a guard dog before, until they were stopped in their tracks by this giant fluffy fur.

Shade started making fun of the overgrown dog and ran around showing off how fast he was.

Susie got angry and bit hit hard, Shadow tripped and was hurt and both managed to run away just in time. Susie was chasing right behind. They jumped into a burrow nearby and were whimpering in pain.

The next morning, after looking out for Susie, and finding him nowhere both Shade and Shadow wandered around and were trying to find their way back home. At midday, after being let to starve the whole night, they spotted the cabbage patch and ran into it and ate all they could before returning to their burrow.

When they went back to the bush where their burrow was, they were welcomed by flat ground.

The hole to the burrow was filled and they could not find any signs of their family. Scared both Shade and Shadow started crying, they blamed each other for not covering the entrance before and were very hurt. They heard Susie from the nearby farm and ran into the mountains.

After days of roaming around, Shade was gathering food while Shadow kept guard. They learnt to lookout for each other. Shade had hurt his leg badly and was hopping around when he saw little marks like the ones Blue used to mark their burrow. Excited he called out to Shadow and together they followed the trail that led them to a small burrow right behind a hollow tree.

When they went into the burrow, they found their mama rabbit hurt and resting, the elder rabbits were taking care of the mama rabbit and were overjoyed to meet the little ones. Shade looked around and could not find papa rabbit. Blue told him that papa rabbit was caught when he was distracting Mrs. Wilsdone, while the others were escaping.

They later found that Mrs. Wilsdone had spotted the burrow after all her plants were bitten and torn. Being furious, she brought a spade and dug into the burrow hitting on mama rabbit. Papa rabbit managed to run the opposite direction, creating a distraction, thus, the others escaped. After hearing this both Shade and Shadow burst into tears and apologized for their mistakes.

The family of rabbits moved into a larger burrow where the elder rabbits brought the food and mama rabbit taught the kids. Papa rabbit was badly injured and had to lose his right hind leg but managed to escape and joined them in their new burrow a year later.

CHAPTER NINE

THE STUDY

Everyday my grandfather would walk into his study and disappear for the whole afternoon. This had been his routine for the past five years after grandma passed away. I had always been curious of where he would go and tried to sneak into his study, only to find it empty every single time.

During my many unsuccessful attempts to shadow him, I have been caught and punished by my mamma. She often tells me, "Tatu, do not disturb your grandpa! It's the only time he takes for himself and he will get very angry if he finds you sneaking in his study." My grandpa always liked his stuff kept at a particular place, so kids were forbidden from entering his study.

The times when I was fortunate enough to get a peak, there was a bookshelf with all kinds of books, some were even kept in cases. The study had a strong wooden table, on which was a table lamp, staplers, and a cup of pencils and pens. Grandpa loved books and writing. He worked as a calligrapher back in his days and people loved him for his talent. Every Christmas, he wrote a heartfelt card to all the members of the family, each one was unique and had one of his favourite poems in it. Everyone would eagerly look forward, each Christmas eve, when he'd finally bring them down from his study.

A few days after my eleventh birthday, everyone in the family had gone to attend a friend's wedding, grandpa had a fever and opted to stay behind to take care of the kids.

Once he had fixed our lunch, he sat down to watch some television. My little sister was fast asleep. I was instructed to do my homework as he was going into his study. He said that he would be back in few minutes and that I could knock hard on his door in case we needed him.

After a few minutes of him leaving the room, I quietly entered his study, to find him vanished into thin air like always. He was nowhere to be found. Having read many adventure books, I came to a conclusion that he had found a passage to another world and was visiting there every day. I paced in the room without making any noise, trying to find any traces of him. Just below the bookshelf was his pen that he carried in his pocket, lying there on the carpet. I picked it up and as I was examining it. I found a little book out of place in one of the lower shelfs. My grandpa is never clumsy and this made me curious, I tried lifting the book and to my utter shock the whole bookshelf moved aside and there was staircase leading down.

A dim light was glowing in the stairs. I carefully stepped on it. The walls of the staircase were decorated with pictures hanging by a thread, pictures of my grandpa and grandma when they were younger. I stood there looking at them for a while, they seemed happy, holding hands or kissing. I wondered if I could have that sparkle in the eye with another human ever. As I was looking at it, I heard a thud. Startled, I ran down the stairs, the room was dimply lit with fairy lights on the either side of the wall. There was a door leading to another room.

I rushed into the room which had a writing table, it was filled with letters and diaries and pens of all kinds, I walked around it to find my grandpa fallen down. I tried to wake him up, with no success, I ran up the stairs to get some water and that's when my mom walked in, seeing me coming out of the study, she was furious and started scolding me. I tried to explain and both my mom and dad rushed down the stairs to help grandpa. He was later taken to hospital where they told us, he had a mild attack and was found at the right time.

After hearing this, my mom hugged me and with tears rolling down her cheek, said that she forgave me this time, for being a nosey brat. Two days later, when grandpa returned home, he called me in his study. I was very nervous. As I stepped inside, I found the bookshelf wide open and grandpa invited me into his secret room down the stairs and for the very first time. I saw the walls had something else other than pictures of my grandparents, there were sticky notes next to each picture and it had a few lines of poems in it.

My grandpa said to me, it was all written by my grandma over the years when she used to sneak the sticky notes between the pages of his book, each time they got into a fight or had an argument, he said, "Every time we had a fight, I would walk into my den and start reading and the very next day I would find a sticky note sneaked into the pages, she always managed to bring a smile on my face.

As long as she was alive, she would gift people poems on Christmas eve. She always reserved the best poems for me, so when she passed away, I surrounded myself with her pictures and handwriting and continued the tradition of gifting a poem. It was my way of remembering her every Christmas.

After listening to his words, I was filled with tears. I never had any great interest in the gift he gave every year since they did not have any money in it and would often toss them in a box and discarded it under my bed, where it stayed unopened, to this day. Seeing me all teared up, grandpa pulled me into his arms, embracing me for the next few mins. I started apologizing to him and he never understood why. He later let me come down to his den and read the poems written by my grandma, which became my favourite hobby every evening after school.

Grandpa would be delighted to see me every day and together we would spend hours talking about how the day went and all the new poems we had read. He even taught me calligraphy and I loved it. Together we made many cards for everyone in the family and waited eagerly for Christmas eve.

CHAPTER TEN

EVERYONE HAS THEIR OWN JOURNEY

Xeto grew up in the willows farm among the other trees that were shiny and green. Xeto was a bit short compared to the trees around him and was often bullied by others. The oldest of them was Gane, a bold tree and everyone looked up to him. Gane would tell Xeto, "Do not worry little one, every tree gets its own place to shine." Hearing this Xeto was delighted, he looked forward to the week when people would come and pick him up.

He had heard stories from the other trees about glittery decoration, shiny balls, and lights. It was something that Xeto had always dreamed off. He wanted to be one of the trees by the window side, decorated with lights that had wrapped gifts resting near his feet.

The fall commenced. Families began the search for Christmas trees. Gane was the first to be sold out. Xeto was sad to part with his dear friend. Yet he was happy that the party had started. Every day many families would walk into the farm, kids running around and pulling the trees. The fathers would carefully examine each tree and once they made up their mind, they would buy a tree and cut it down with the kids cheering up.

A week had passed and most of the trees were sold out. Xeto was heartbroken and sad, no one had noticed him except for the little kids. They would run around Xeto asking if they could have him. And every time, he would get excited, only to be rejected by their father for being too short.

On the day when Xeto had lost all his hope of finding a new home, he was sadly looking at the ground, missing Gane. A small puppy was wagging his tail right under the little tree. Xeto looked up, a kid was chasing the little puppy. He was wearing a woollen sweater and torn gloves. His dad was right behind him, signed and asked if this was the tree that the puppy loved. Both the kid and the puppy were jumping up and down.

Xeto was happy to be picked up at last. He was then pulled on to their sledge and started their long journey home. After one hour of travelling, they came to a little hut with a fence around it. Mom walked out to help dad with the tree and put it near the sofa.

Xeto looked around. It wasn't the window side he had always hoped to be at. This was a rather small hut with a single bedroom and a tiny hall with a fireplace, yet, Xeto was very happy as the kid and the dog ran around to pick up their toys, trying to decorate the tree. The dad helped them to hang toys on the tree. An hour later, Xeto was decorated with candy canes and ginger bread. The kid also hanged his little teddy bear and the dog brought his bone to make it a part of the decoration.

That night the dad brought a little present and put it right under the tree. He looked up at Xeto and thanked him for growing up so small, because he was not able to afford a bigger tree. Since Xeto was small, people had ignored him, and the shop keeper agreed for a cheaper price.

Though he did not find an expensive window, Xeto was very happy to be a part of this beautiful family. He now understood Gane's words, "Every tree has its own place to shine."

CHAPTER ELEVEN

Aren't We All Strangers Until, We've Met?

Sri and his friends had planned a short trip for the weekend. Ever since he told people where he was going, they warned him to be safe, advising him that people at Kanva were cunning and would deceive him without a second thought. Although Sri had never visited that place, he kept an open mind and started the journey with his friends. To reach Kanva, they had to travel by train for a whole day.

Six days into the journey, all five friends were having a good time and most of the cash they carried was spent already. They had to take a ferry ride to reach their next destination. The ferryman asked for the cash and they did not have any. They agreed to find an ATM once they've reached the other side, although they were total strangers, the ferryman took them on his boat and also offered his bicycle to reach the ATM.

Once they came back with the money, they thanked the ferryman for his trust and paid him generously. Sri asked him why he trusted them while they were total strangers and could have walked off without paying. To this, the ferryman replied, "Aren't we all strangers until we have met? People surprise you kid, it doesn't hurt to trust, even if you had walked away, I would have simply smiled and went on helping people."

"Just because a person cheats us, it does not mean that everyone is the same." After hearing his words, Sri was deeply moved, thinking about how his people have warned him before. He thought they were being ignorant. The ferryman later gave them coconuts from his farm and provided them meal before they continued with the journey.

The friends travelled around Kanva the next day and reached a dhabba for lunch. When they sat down talking about the previous day's events, Steph who was seated in the next table heard their conversation and introduced himself as a solo traveller. Steph then went on to narrate an incident a few years back when he had visited the same place with his friends. He said, "We had a good time during the trip and were on our way back home, where we had an accident on the highway, we were out of cash and did not know what to do, a stranger who was in the scene noticed us and came to our help, he also spoke our language and understood that we were just students and did not carry the amount to fix the car and other damages. He did not hesitate even a minute before offering us ten thousand rupees. He gave us his phone number and account details and only asked us to pay it back once we'd reached home safely. We were total strangers and the only thing that connected us was the language, we could have gotten the money and ran off, yet he did not worry about any of it and came to our aid."

"We were just students then, frightened and with no clue of what to do, we were aimlessly wandering in the road and this man helped us. I cannot forget him till this date, once we reached home, we wired his money and also thanked him for his kindness. We keep in touch with him even now, it was the most frightening and amazing experience we had."

After listening to the story Sri's opinion of people changed completely. He realised there is more than one perspective to things and there are more good people in the world than bad ones. The short trip he took with his friends let him meet beautiful souls and he carried the experience in his heart forever.

(Based on a true incident).

CHAPTER TWELVE

LITTLE FAYE

The most beautiful place in Wolfslair was the big banyan tree in the centre of the town.

It was huge and had all kinds of shops in it. The first floors had cafes and restaurants, the second floor had theatres, and the third floor had parlours.

It also had lifts made of rope and tyre. There were many trees around the great banyan tree, although most of it was houses, there was a tree which was so tall like a lighthouse, it was their watch tower.

Two wolves were stationed there around the clock to lookout for any sight of intruders. All the trees in the village were connected by canopy bridges. The village was protected by rocks and covered from the world with thick forests. No one in a hundred years had stepped into the village except for the wolves.

Mr. Tristy owned an ice-cream shop in the big banyan tree and everyday many wolves visited his shop from morning till noon to have a cool ice lolly. One Sunday, Mr. Tristy and his help, little Faye, were on their way to collect ice for their shop. When they were busy gathering ice, they did not notice the little mouse that sneaked into their big basket and burrowed itself a small hole to take a nap. Once they had collected enough ice for the week, they walked all the way back to Wolfslair. After the usual greetings at the watch tower their baskets were examined, since the wolves at the tower knew Mr. Tristy well, they only took a glance at the basket and let him in.

As soon as Mr. Tristy reached his shop, he put the baskets into the storage room and went on with his busy day. The time went by and the little mouse woke up from its long nap. It came out and looked around to find itself locked inside the storage room. It was very hungry and wanted to find its way out. It ran around the room, only found baskets of ice stored. The mouse then climbed a ladder to take a look at the top shelfs and to his relief he found an ice-cream cake, that was made and left there to rest. The little mouse hungrily gobbled the whole cake. Tired of eating such a desert for the first time in his life, he went back to sleep again.

Thirty minutes later, a big wolf named, Gabbot and his kid walked into the ice cream shop to receive the ice cream cake that they had ordered. Little Faye was instructed to bring it out, but once he went into the storage room, he was shocked to see the empty tray on the top shelf. However, he was in awe at the little creature that was snoozing right next to the tray.

Faye had never seen a mouse in his whole life and this little creature fascinated him. He stood there looking at the mouse for quite a long time, Mr. Tristy was getting impatient waiting for little Faye and he wanted to see what took him this long, he walked towards the storage room, when little Faye heard the footsteps, he knew that the mouse was in great trouble. He had taken a liking to the mouse and quickly grabbed him and shoved him into his pocket, the little mouse was scared at the sudden event, started struggling in Faye's hands. Faye assured him to stay there without any noise. Mr. Tristy walked in and gasped at the empty tray, he got angry on little Faye, thinking it was him who had eaten the cake.

Faye then reminded him that he was with Mr. Tristy all along and there was not enough time for him to have done such a dreadful deed. Mr. Tristy was so confused and furious, he stormed out of the room and called upon a few wolves to search for the thief. He then walked toward Gabbot and apologized, insisting he would get another cake ready and deliver it to his tree house. Though his kid had started crying at this point, Gabbot comforted him, agreed and walked out.

The shop was closed and all the wolves were looking out for the thief, they searched through the halls of the great tree, the parlours and the cafes, two wolves came in to identify the paw prints but they did not find any as Faye has erased the prints of little mouse, the canopy bridges were filled with wolves moving up and down searching every nook and corner.

The little mouse who had been watching all this from the pocket of Faye was terrified. He knew he had messed up, he was weeping silently. Little Faye shushed him. He quietly slipped through the chaos and almost made it to the rocks. As he walked past the watch tower, he was stopped by two wolves who enquired where he was going. He later told them about the incident and that he was instructed to bring more ice, they asked him why he was alone and little Faye told them his master was busy searching for the thief, convinced by the answer the wolves let him pass.

Once they were out on the other side of the thick forest, Little Faye grabbed little mouse out of his pocket and set him free. The mouse thanked little Faye for his kindness and promised to be his friend.

Little Faye walked back to Wolfslair, with more ice and Mr. Tristy made another ice cream cake. They did not find out the thief even though Mr. Tristy never gave up the search, he also never left the store for collecting ice from that day. It was little Faye's job to collect the ice.

Every time, little Faye went on his mission, he always came back late, only to be scolded by Mr. Tristy. In spite of the punishment, little Faye was cheerful on his walks as he was usually met by the mouse right outside the rocks and they spent the whole day together talking about stories. Faye would bring treats and little mouse offer him grapes from the nearby farm. They stayed best buddies though the years.

CHAPTER THIRTEEN

EXPECTATIONS

Sunday morning! I was very excited. As the alarm went off, I sprang to my feet. I knew this was going to be an extraordinary day, since I was going to meet my favourite band. The Jutebox!! Listening to their songs every single day, pestering my parents for a whole month, I had secured two tickets for their show this evening.

Molly and I had picked up our dresses a week before. She was my best friend, who was also crazy about Jutebox. We had planned everything beforehand, we were going to be there a whole hour prior to the show, to be able to meet any of the band members.

Jutebox was the upcoming band in our small town. Every week their tickets were sold out. Apart from their songs, the band members had stolen the hearts of every girl in the town. Especially Jean, he had long hair till his shoulders, he played guitar and was the lead singer. He had everything a girl can dream of!

The show was at four p. m., time doesn't fly when you're waiting impatiently for something. I did not have enough patience to wait until four and had gotten ready by one p. m., my mom laughed at me as I never got ready early for any celebration or outing. She called it a miracle! Another hour passed by slowly, I heard my friend honking loudly in the street, I grabbed my shoes and ran to greet her.

Thirty minutes later we reached the venue. To our utter disappointment, it was empty. I and my friend were so excited about the day that we did not check updates about the show, apparently someone in the band had fallen ill and the show was cancelled at the last minute. We made our way into the club, the stage was not set, and the chairs had no one in it. Yet we heard voices from the back, hoping to stumble onto any of the team members, we peaked into the backstage.

There they were! Seated around in chairs and talking, it was Jean who noticed us peaking in. He waved at us asking us to join. They then went on to apologize for the inconvenience and since we had come all the way, they promised to give us free pass for their next show. It was all like a dream. We were seated next to the Jutebox!

Talking and sharing their sandwich. Molly and I spent two hours chatting with them, most of my time was spent with me crushing hard on Jean, and he did notice it and smiled back at me. I screamed in joy. We then parted with them after taking a few pictures.

On the way back to our car, both of us did not utter a single word. The minute we were seated inside the car, we were screaming at the top of our lungs!

At night I pulled out my diary to make notes of the best day of my life. How expectations were met with disappointments and every disappointment had a brighter side to it. If we had made to the actual show, we would still have had a blast, standing in the crowd and screaming our lungs out. Yet today, we got to spend two hours with the people we admired and had crush and we shared a sandwich with them and this day would always be remembered to the end of my lovely life as the most precious day ever.

CHAPTER FOURTEEN

MR. SCHEMENZER

Mr. Schemenzer is a Persian breed, snow white, twelve inches tall, mysterious yet a friendly cat, gifted to me by my husband three years ago. He walks down the halls demanding attention and treats. He loves to play with my son, when he's back from school. His normal routine consists of waking up at seven, crawling in for a nap with my husband, shooing me out of my own bed.

Later, he enjoyed eating the breakfast that I put out for him. He would wake up my son and once everyone leave for work. He resumes his spot on the windowsill and carefully watches the street, until my son comes back from school. He goes out the kitty door every time he sees the mailman stops by.

Today, when he was looking out his window, Mr. Schemenzer started meowing, he later went out the kitty door, as I was washing the dishes back in the kitchen, I heard him meowing loudly, I assumed he's trying to scare away the neighbour's dog.

Few minutes later, Mr. Schemenzer walked into the kitchen and started pulling my apron. I understood he was trying to get my attention, I asked him what it was. He then walked towards the window and began meowing again. I took a peek through the window and saw a lady bent down in front of our house, she seemed in pain. I quickly walked out, calling out if she was in the need of help. I could see that she was pregnant and wet all over.

She then managed to tell me that her water had broken and contractions started. I tried to bring her into my house before calling for help. We hadn't made past the steps when she collapsed on the front porch. I ran in and dialled 911. Made her comfortable on the front porch with pillows and waited for the ambulance which arrived after ten minutes.

The first responders were unable to transfer her since the baby had already started crowing. I realised that woman was going to deliver the baby in my front porch. I ran in and brought some fresh towels. Mr. Schemenzer, stayed on the porch witnessing everything that was happening, he was very quiet and stayed out of everyone's way.

Within the next five minutes, the baby was born, wrapped in clean towel. The woman was then taken into the ambulance to be transported along with the baby to the nearby hospital.

Once the ambulance was out of sight, I sat down on the porch, everything that happened felt like a dream. The events of the whole afternoon were running through my head, Mr. Schemenzer walked to my side and leaned on me. I was very proud of him. Had he not dragged me out of the kitchen, the woman might have fainted before my house.

After cleaning up the porch, I walked in to call my husband to tell him everything that happened. Mr. Schemenzer climbed up his windowsill and continued his watch over the neighbourhood as if it was just another activity ticked off his daily routine.

CHAPTER FIFTEEN

To Love a Little More

I keep starring into his eyes as he stands there talking to the crowd. He's Ajay, a stand-up comedian, I've met him in an online app, where he performed shows with random strangers during lockdown, he'd always managed to make every single one of them burst into laughter. It was his profile picture that made me stay. He's the dream guy of every girl. He wore a black shirt, folded up to sleeves with a bright smile.

Instant crush mode activated, I stayed listening to his voice, I would rush online every time I had a notification that he was there, stalked him, and now landed at his live show. It's my third show so far, but I haven't got the courage to tell him how I felt about him.

I've tortured my friends to go with me. Every week, I found a reason to be there, an excuse to text him and was over the clouds every time he replied.

Should we always tell the person how we feel about them? Even when we know they might not be interested? Too many questions passing in and out of the doors in my brain and I decided to just, love him a little more.

Every week I showed up, laughed out at his jokes, talked with him a few minutes after the show, smiled like an idiot, loose myself in his eyes, and came back the following week to do this all over again.

This has become my routine every Sunday. Throughout the week, I look forward to this day just to be able to look into his eyes again.

One Friday night, just as we were having a game of truth or dare among my friends, I was foolish to choose dare and was asked to propose to my crush. I was scared, yet did it in the only way I knew how. I wrote him a poem, it went as follows,

You light up my skies
Like a thousand fireflies,
Make me dance around
Like a cluster of daffodils.

You make the breeze,
Stop and whisper your name,
Your sweet smiles, glistening eyes,
I see you, not just a fragment,
Of my imagination,
I see you bold, fierce,
Grasping your dreams
And riding wild.

And like a leaf, falling off
Gently, drifting away,
I find myself
Drifting towards you,
All over again.

And I waited, a long forty-five minutes for him to see the message. When he did, he sent me a thank you, with a smiling emoji. I didn't really expect much of a reply, yet a thank you hurt me more than I realised. Still, all I wanted to do was let him know I had a crush on him and that was it. So, I sent back a smiley. Maybe little crushes are meant to stay as little crushes and that's what makes our life a bit interesting. I learned to put on a smile and moved on.

CHAPTER SIXTEEN

THE HALLOWEEN

That day I learnt behind every mask is a totally different person. Villains can be found hiding behind a hero's mask, a kind person might be perceived as arrogant due to his looks.

It was Halloween day, we had a party at my friend's house. I had begged my parents to let me go, they agreed but under the condition that I was to be accompanied by my little sister Tyler.

I was excited to be there and said yes instantly. My sister had dressed up as bunny and I did not want anything to do with her. So, as soon as we left home, I walked her to the neighbour's place and left her with the kids there so that I could spend time with my friends.

It got pretty late in the evening, I set out to find the neighbours kids. I found them near one of the houses counting on the candies they each had got that evening, but my sister was nowhere to be found. When I asked them, they replied that Tyler had just left. I was now panicking a bit at the thought that I had lost my sister and I would be killed by my parents if I did not find her.

For the next ten minutes, I walked around searching for my sister. I had also called my friends to help me find her.

We had spread out and were searching for her when the neighbour's kids also joined in. The kids told us about a man in a superman suit walking around the neighbouring asking if the kids needed a pet. Now I was really sweating and scared about my sister. As we were talking to the kids, one of my friends called me to inform that they had found a bunny dress abandoned near the big banyan tree.

I rushed there to confirm that it was my sister's dress. We had no clue where she was gone. As we were searching around the area, a motorist who was seated with a bunch of other bikers called us to find out what we were doing.

One of my friends told them that my sister was missing and we were trying to find her. She also asked them if they had seen any little kid with curly hair walking all by herself. As we were talking, my little sister dashed at us from the middle of the bikers group. I was so relieved and ran to hug and held her in my arms.

By this time, we had already informed our parents. They found their way to us. They saw us together, hugged us both, and scolded me for letting her off my sight. They went up to the bikers to thank them for taking care of my sister.

The next day, I stayed home as I was grounded. During breakfast, Tyler went on to tell us how she was standing alone not knowing where to find me, the man in the superman suit had approached her and offered to help find me. My sister almost followed him to his car, when they guy was interrupted by the bikers who were doubtful of his intentions. Just as they had expected, once he saw a group of bikers, he bolted leaving my sister behind.

On hearing the story, I began crying uncontrollably and apologized to my sister and parents. As I was frightened, they held me in their arms and comforted me. From that day on, I never let my little sister venture alone. Also I always looked out for little kids when they were lost.

We later found the bikers and invited them for lunch in our backyard. The story soon reached to everyone in the town and all the neighbours pitched in with their special dishes. We were able to put together a feast for the bikers, as a gratitude for their kindness and love.

TO LOVE A LITTLE MORE

CHAPTER SEVENTEEN

HERE WE SELL SMILES

A row of six houses, all stacked together, covered with snow, each of these houses had windows that looked towards the lake, Often, people left their extra sweaters hanging on the fences for the homeless and the needy to make use of it.

The people in these houses would leave food, all wrapped and kept inside the box, at the stand near the fence, for anyone who was hungry, they had left a note that read: "We sell smiles".

I passed by these houses on my way to work, wondering what the note meant. Every now and then, I get to see someone from the house, walking towards the fence, to leave a scarf or a hot meal for the homeless. I've always wondered what they did for a living, what jobs they had, and what were their earnings. I did give for the poor every once in a while, but these people do that every day.

One such day, as I was taking a stroll, I witnessed a woman leaving a hat inside the box. I walked towards her smiling, seeing me, she waved back. I introduced myself as Sam. She invited me in, for a hot cup of coffee. The living room was very spacious. They had a cat that was resting comfortably on a cushion near the sofa. We started to chat. As curious as I was, I started bombarding her with questions on why these people kept helping others and how they managed to do that every day.

The lady smiled, she introduced herself as Kiera. She told me that Marge the lady who lives next door used to have a commotion every first Saturday as they go out for shopping. When asked about it, she told them she would use coupons to shop. At first, we all were judging her, thinking she was a penny pincher. Later, we saw what she did. Every week, she would leave some canned food at the fence with a note for any homeless person to treat themselves.

We also found out that she would give groceries to the orphanage nearby. Seeing this, we were inspired by her and also collected coupons to help her, that was five years back. We now do our shopping spree every alternative month and all the housewives here make sure to stock up with the necessary items every month. This has not only helped the homeless around, but also gave us enough, that the children at the school nearby did not have to worry about lunch money as all the groceries were being donated to them every week.

Hearing this, I was amazed how much these people have come together as a community and how well they looked after each other. After sipping on a good cup of hot chocolate, I walked out to find an old man taking off the hat from the box and waving to the women at the door. Feeling warm, in body and heart, I walked back home.

That evening, I left a box at the fence with some old clothes and a note that read: "Here we sell smiles."

CHAPTER EIGHTEEN

HOPE THE HAPPY ELF

Every Christmas eve, there was a contest held among the elves. The one who wins it, gets to ride the sledge, help out Santa and also gets to choose his favourite reindeer. Lumpy, Clumsy, and Hope were brothers. Since they were little, they have heard stories of elves who had won the contest, the adventure they go on and the reindeer they own.

Lumpy being tall for his age knew it would be him winning this year, he had made sure to get on Santa's good graces, offering him a cup of hot coffee every time he was in the town.

Clumsy did not bother for the price. He was just excited to go to the contest to see other elves compete. Hope lived in the clouds, talking about fairy dust and how they could create sparkles in the gift wrappers. He was nicknamed Cloudy.

On the day of the contest, Hope was barely scrapping through to the next level. Lumpy however had made good progress. Lumpy being tall, could look through the crowd, he managed to find a shortcut to reach his target easily and would come back with this prize in minutes. Hope had to go through the crowd, searching every nook and corner.

The last round was to feed a reindeer and to ride it. Lumpy tried to feed a carrot, but the reindeer he chose was not in a good mood. He started kicking and running away. Hope though was very scared yet amazed at the creature, walked slowly in front of it, cautious not to startle it. Once he stood there in the front, he started talking to the majestic animal, like a friend, he was awed at the creature and tried to stroke its side. The reindeer who was observing him for a while, allowed him touch it.

Hope squealed in joy, all the elves watching were amazed. Clumsy was at the edge of the seat, Santa was pleased. The reindeers have high standards, for any elf who interacts with them, only the purest of hearts, a believer in true magic will be able to successfully mount them.

That day, even though he wasn't tall, or great, Hope was filled with magic, his eyes sparkled when he looked at the creature and the reindeer let Hope ride on him.

The minute Hope got on the reindeer, it started galloping and slowly lifted off. All the elves were cheering loudly. Hope was holding tightly, filled with laughter and excitement, he waved at the elves as he passed them.

Hope had a warm welcome by Santa when he dismounted the reindeer. That year, Hope won the contest. He chose the same reindeer to be his loyal friend. Lumpy was disappointed at first, slowly realised his mistake of finding shortcuts to succeed. But he was happy for Hope.

That night, Hope travelled with Santa on his cart. They flew over the top of house after house, village after village, dropping gifts through chimneys. Every time a gift was dropped, Hope would say a simple spell that made the wrapper shine in the dark, with little sparkles like the stars in the sky. He even managed to leave them a little note.

On Christmas morning, when the kids ran down the stairs, they found the little parcels sparkling right under the tree. There was laughter in the air, children jumping up and down, tears of joy and smiles all over the town. Every gift that was unwrapped had a little bell left behind by Hope. The note read: "Anytime you lose your footing, when things get tough, ring the bell, Hope will find you, wherever you are."

"Sprinkle love into the world,
Let the wind spread it wide
Let the rain soak it up,
And sprout out little smiles."
-Dino
(Priyanga.M.Srinivasan)

www.ingramcontent.com/pod-product-compliance
Lightning Source LLC
Chambersburg PA
CBHW031423160726
47993CB00003B/1369